BUTTS ARE EVERYWHERE

Words by JONATHAN STUTZMAN

Pictures by HEATHER FOX

putnam

G. P. Putnam's Sons

(side)

To Mr. Huck:
For kicking my butt in the right direction
—H.F.

G. P. PUTNAM'S SONS
An imprint of Penguin Random House LLC, New York

Text copyright © 2020 by Jonathan Stutzman
Illustrations copyright © 2020 by Heather Fox

G. P. Putnam's Sons is a registered trademark of Penguin Random House LLC.

Visit us online at penguinrandomhouse.com

Library of Congress Cataloging-in-Publication Data
Names: Stutzman, Jonathan, author. | Fox, Heather, illustrator.
Title: Butts are everywhere / Jonathan Stutzman; illustrated by Heather Fox.
Description: New York: G. P. Putnam's Sons, [2020] | Summary: "A celebration of one of our most useful
(and hilarious) body parts"—Provided by publisher.
Identifiers: LCCN 2020000349 (print) | LCCN 2020000350 (ebook) | ISBN 9780525514510 (hardback) |
ISBN 9780525514541 (kindle edition) | ISBN 9780525514527 (ebook)
Subjects: CYAC: Buttocks—Fiction. | Flatulence—Fiction. | Humorous stories.
Classification: LCC PZ7.1.S798 Bu 2020 (print) | LCC PZ7.1.S798 (ebook) | DDC [E]—dc23
LC record available at https://lccn.loc.gov/2020000349
LC ebook record available at https://lccn.loc.gov/2020000350

Manufactured in China by RR Donnelley Asia Printing Solutions Ltd.
ISBN 9780525514510
1 3 5 7 9 10 8 6 4 2

Design by Marikka Tamura
Text set in Atelier Sans ITC Std
The art for this book was created digitally.

Butts are everywhere.

Tiny butts.
Big butts.

Smooth butts
and prickly butts,

hairy butts
and wrinkly butts.

Every sort of butt you can imagine.

Who has a butt? That's a good question.

Moms do,

dads do,

brothers and sisters and
grandpappies do.

Even your friends have tushies.

But you know that already. What you may not know is that butts have many names.

CAKES

BUM-BUM

HAUNCHES

Booty

RUMP

CAN

Booty

TUSH

BACKSIDE

HAMS DERRIERE

REAR

Buttocks is the scientific name for your backside.

Every great human in
the history of the world
has had a tush.
They come in every
size and color.

Your behind is right behind you. If you don't see yours,
that might mean you're sitting on it.

Heinies are very useful. They're not just
silly words or something to crack jokes about.
You see, cheeks make wonderful seats.

Whether you're riding a bike . . .

reading a book . . .

or creating a masterpiece . . .

. . . your butt cheeks give you
the soft, cushy padding you need
to sit comfortably.

The muscles in your pompis are powerful.

Your gluteus maximus will propel you
into the air if you jump, and your buns
will catch you if you fall.

No matter how you swing it,
your caboose has your back.

Humans are not the only ones with buns.
Nature is full of them.
Some animal dupas are enormous.
They can smush you flat if you aren't careful.
Others you can barely see.

Animal tooters can be hairy.
Colorful. Prickly. Cuddly.
And downright lovable.

Some animals have hindquarters that aren't butts.
Dolphins. Worms. Jellies. Whales.

No-Butt CLUB!

If a blue whale had a keister,
it would be the biggest booty on Earth.
Land or sea.

Animals use their rears in many strange and interesting ways:

To get to know each other.

To sleep.

To breathe.

Fun fact:
Manatees toot from their tuchus to help them swim faster.

Another fun fact:
I toot.
You toot.
Old ladies at tea parties toot.
We all toot.
It's science!

Our patooties are quite the tooters.

Every fart cannon has a distinct sound.

Some hum softly.

Some

KaPLOOF!

loud and proud.

Believe me when I say a pīgu
can turn into a *pee-ew!*
really fast.

But do not fear!
It is perfectly natural
and healthy for
your hams to oink.

(Just remember to say "excuse me!" when they do.)

There are BILLIONS of bum-bums on our grand planet. More bum-bums than you or I could ever count.

1.. 2.. 3...

And it doesn't matter if your backside
is round, pointy, tiny, huge, prickly,
hairy, loud, purple, pink, or
some curious mix of every color . . .

your keister, your dupa,
your wonderful can, is perfect
and unique just as it is.

Just like you,

YOUR BUTT IS

AWESOME!